GILL VICKERY

Illustrated by ALEKSEI BITSKOFF

BLOOMSBURY EDUCATION
AN IMPRINT OF BLOOMSBURY
LONDON OXFORD NEW YORK NEW DELHI SYDNEY

CONTENTS

Chapter One	Back to Franklin's Emporium	7
Chapter Two	The Invisible Cat	16
Chapter Three	Mirror, Mirror	22
Chapter Four	Paws 4 Thought	31
Chapter Five	Fading Away	40
Chapter Six	The Poltergeist	46
Chapter Seven	The Seven Mysteries of Golden Bay	55
Chapter Eight	The Magicians' Battle	66
Chapter Nine	The Installation	71
Chapter Ten	Disaster!	77
Chapter Eleven	Brothers	85

Chapter One
BACK TO FRANKLIN'S EMPORIUM

'I'll see you again, soon.'

The voice echoed in my head as I waited for the lift in Franklin's Emporium.

When the old liftman had said those words to me eight months ago I'd almost laughed. I knew there was no way – ever – I was going to come back to the seaside town of Golden Bay and its huge, run-down old department store, Franklin's Emporium. Yet here I was, with my mum, waiting to get into the lift.

The lift pinged and the doors slid open. The liftman pulled aside the black metal grille and Mum went in, trying and failing to see over the pile of *Fran's Fancies* cake boxes in her arms. I stuck as close as possible to her and stared at the

floor. I did not want to make eye contact with the liftman.

Mum nudged me with an elbow. 'Move over, there's plenty of room.'

I shuffled grudgingly away, about five centimetres.

'Top floor, Terrace Restaurant, please,' Mum said in her chirpy way.

The lift glided upwards. I sneaked a glance at the liftman. He didn't look any different from how I remembered him. He still wore a smart blue uniform with gold epaulettes and a pocket embroidered with three gold crowns. He stood, tall and gaunt, in his corner, bright eyes peering at me from under huge eyebrows like a hedge in need of trimming. I thought he might say, 'Nice to see you again,' but he didn't speak a word until we got to the top floor.

'Terrace restaurant,' he announced and opened the doors on the busy restaurant.

I nipped in front of Mum. 'I'll guide you.' I steered her out.

'Thank you,' she called over her shoulder to the liftman.

'You're welcome, Madam,' he said in his cracked old voice. The doors shut and the lift glided downwards.

'Strange old man,' Mum said.

'Too right,' I muttered, leading Mum through the tables to the counter at the far end where a jolly, fattish man was sifting through papers.

He beamed with a grin like a half-moon when he saw us. 'Ah, the cakes – the wonderful cakes!' He trundled out from behind the counter.

'To the kitchen with these.' He took the boxes from Mum and whisked away, backwards, through a pair of swing doors. 'Come!' he bellowed.

Mum shook her head in amused exasperation. 'You don't need to stay. Charles wants to sort out orders for tomorrow and it'll take a while. He's very particular about my cakes.'

She rummaged in her purse for some money. 'Get some treats for Cesare.'

Cesare is her new kitten and she's besotted with him.

'Get a toy for him as well. There's plenty to choose from in the pet shop unit.'

When Franklin's Emporium closed long ago, it became neglected and run down. Then it was sold, re-opened and let out in units. There were all kinds: cafes and coffee shops, second-hand book shops, furniture and toy shops. There was once a haberdashery, though that disappeared last summer.

The pet shop unit, *Paws 4 Thought*, was on the ground floor but there was no way I was going to take the lift. I walked down all seven flights of stairs so as to avoid the liftman. He was a kind of wizard and I wasn't going to risk getting involved in his magic, not after what happened last summer.

I came out in the grand, marble-floored lobby supported by pillars sculpted with nymphs and fauns. Right in the middle of the vast space was a huge cube of red fabric. It was covering scaffolding that stuck out at the top. As I passed it I heard my brother Ben's voice and a lot of hammering and banging. My brothers were artists and this was one of their installations. I grinned. The inhabitants of Golden Bay were going to get a surprise when the covers came off.

The pet shop unit was tucked away in a corner, on the other side of the lobby. A lot of the units and pop-up shops arrived overnight like mushrooms and disappeared just as suddenly. *Paws 4 Thought* had appeared like that, materialising the day before Cesare sauntered up our garden path and turned my mum's brain to mush.

Mum had picked the kitten up and done the cooing thing. I knew he'd cast a spell on her when she instantly forgot about her new bakery

project and went hunting for food to stop the kitten's tragic mewing. Up till then Mum had been totally obsessed with setting up her cake and bakery business, *Fran's Fancies*. That was one of the reasons we'd come to live in Golden Bay.

She was going to call the kitten Misty but Dad called him Cesare after some evil old Italian duke, and it stuck – for good reason. Cesare was a complete tyrant: he tore the curtains, scratched the furniture, weed on the carpets and even chewed up my school project. Mum had to write a letter to my teacher saying the cat ate my homework.

For a creature that was adorable – all round blue eyes and smoky grey fur – he had an evil heart. It was the cutesy-pie kitten's fault that the invisicat came to stay and refused to budge.

Paws 4 Thought was bigger than it looked from the outside. The main part was stacked with sacks of cat litter and dog biscuits, birdseed and racks of collars, poop-scoops and bird feeders. The rest was divided into four separate areas: one for fish, one for rodents, one for birds and a private, curtained off area at the back.

The pet shop owner was poking around as if he was trying to find something. When he saw me he

flapped his hand irritably, said, 'I'll be with you in a minute,' and started pulling boxes off a shelf and peering behind them.

I didn't mind. It was the Easter holidays and I had time to waste.

Like some other units in Franklin's, *Paws 4 Thought* was strange. It was gloomy, lit by dismal, dusty bulbs. The only bright illumination came from occasional flashes of coloured light from around the edges of the sagging black drapes at the back of the shop.

The pets had fresh food and water but their roomy cages were made of curly, wrought iron metal with bolts and cogs and elaborate locks on the doors. If they'd had wheels they'd have rolled about on their own as if a mad scientist had wound them up. Inside their ornate cages the animals and birds were creepily silent.

In the shadowy aquarium, fish sailed monotonously back and forth in illuminated tanks, occasionally diving down to ruined gothic castles, sunken airships and skulls with jaws that opened and shut. I liked those. I picked up a display skull and was feeding it a simpering mermaid when a jingling noise made me turn.

It was the pet shop owner. He was short and thin with an ordinary face except for the fact

it was very, very pale and he had huge ears. An earring, shaped like a snake eating its own tail, hung from the left lobe. He wore a sort of saggy dressing gown in balding black velvet. He was clutching a blue cat collar with three large bells on it. That's where the jingling noise came from.

'Have you lost a cat?' I asked, putting the mermaid back on the shelf.

'None of your business,' he snapped through a mean little mouth. 'What do you want?'

'I'm looking for cat toys,' I said.

'You won't find any in here. Try over there.'

He pointed to a rack near the counter. His finger was encircled by a large ring embossed with another snake.

I went over and browsed. I chose a treat dispenser shaped like a mouse's head. It had a giant pink nose and ears, and holes in the sides for biscuits to fall out of when the cat batted it around. Cesare would like that – he was keen on battering things. I picked up a box of meaty snacks as well.

Two customers came in and I went back to the fish room while the owner was serving them. I thought about feeding the mermaid to a plastic shark. Maybe set up a tug-of-war with the skull?

Maybe not. I didn't want to get a bad reputation, not now Mum and Dad had units here and it was only a couple of days to the boys' exhibition.

I bent down and looked at a blue and gold Siamese fighting fish drifting aimlessly round and round its tank. Staring at me from the other side of the tank was a pair of slanted yellow eyes. I nearly leapt out of my skin.

The eyes vanished.

Strange.

As I leaned forward for a closer look I dropped the box of treats. It rattled. Instantly the eyes appeared again. I picked up the box and shook it experimentally. The eyes moved around the side of the tank to the front, stopped and looked right at me.

When I said, 'the eyes moved,' that's exactly what happened. The eyes. No body, only the eyes. And a loud throbbing purr.

Chapter Two
THE INVISIBLE CAT

I opened the box and shook a few treats onto the ledge in front of the fish tank. The eyes lowered in their direction and I heard a faint, 'sniff, sniff, sniff.' After a brief pause the biscuits disappeared, one by one. When they'd gone, the eyes floated upwards and turned back on me. The purring grew louder.

Very cautiously I stretched out my hand. The eyes retreated sharply. I put a couple of treats on my palm and held it out. The eyes approached and hovered above my hand.

Rasp, rasp. It was all I could do to stop myself from shrieking. A rough tongue – a rough, invisible tongue – had licked up the food and carefully lapped up the fragments.

I held out more treats and while the eyes and tongue were busy I felt the space around them.

I touched fur. I stroked it and felt a furry head, a furry back, a long furry tail, a happily vibrating throat. The only problem was, I couldn't see any of them. I was stroking an invisible cat.

It began to sniff at my jacket sleeve and the purr got louder. I think it could smell Cesare – he'd chewed my cuff that morning.

A hand gripped my shoulder and pulled me away. It was the pet shop owner still holding the jingly collar. He must've been trying to find the invisible cat.

'What are you up to?' he said.

I shook off his hand. I wasn't going to have a conversation about an invisible cat. Invisibility was impossible and if I was wrong about what he was searching for I'd look a complete fool.

'I was watching the fighting fish while you were busy. What did you think I was doing?'

'Messing around in my shop. Get out.'

That was harsh. If I hadn't been worried about my family working in Franklin's I'd have argued my corner. Instead I just shrugged and left.

Outside, I turned to look back at Franklin's Emporium. It rose high above me; seven storeys of white stone with blue granite carved into archways above the doors and windows. Blue and white

paintwork sparkled in the sun, though this didn't hide the fact it was cracked and peeling. I still loved Franklin's, inside and out, for looking like something out of a fantasy novel – all that marble, alabaster and gilt – all those soaring columns and ethereal statues. The only reason I didn't love it as much as I used to was because I knew that if you weren't very careful weird things happened to you inside. Like meeting invisible cats – which were impossible.

I thought about the cat as I walked home and hardly noticed passing the pier and the harbour. As I turned onto a narrow cobbled street leading up to my house, a sudden furious barking made me jump.

'Stupid dog,' I muttered at the springer spaniel bouncing up and down behind a garden wall like a demented jack-in-a-box. Its brown and white head kept appearing, mouth open, pink tongue flapping – boing, boing, boing. Its wide eyes, rolling like marbles, focussed on the top of the wall. There was nothing there. It had got itself all worked up over nothing.

I ran the rest of the way home and burst through the door, stomach rumbling.

I checked my watch. Lunchtime already?

There was nobody about. Mum and Ben were still at Franklin's, Dad was in his workshop at the bottom of the garden and Sam was in the studio on the top floor.

We had two kitchens at home. One was for Mum's business; that got regularly inspected to make sure she was following all the hygiene and safety rules. Only Mum went in there. It was even out of bounds to Cesare. I went into the family kitchen, made two mugs of tea and a pile of tuna and mayo sandwiches. I loaded them on a tray, added a couple of fat wedges from one of Mum's buttercream cakes and went down the garden to Dad's workshop.

It was a big garden – really big – with a huge pond and a hedge maze. There was also a small wood with a kitchen garden behind it. Dad's workshop was there, built over the site of an old shed that burned down last year. I got the blame even though it was my horrible cousin, Maisie, who did it. We didn't talk about it.

I liked the big workshop. It smelled of varnish and paint, and motes of golden sawdust floated in the light streaming from the windows in the roof. Dad did his woodturning and carpentry in there. He'd stopped for a while to fit out Mum's unit,

now he was busy building up stock. He made bowls and goblets, little stools and coffee tables, and polished up driftwood to sell in his unit at Franklin's.

'Hi Dad.' I put the tray of tea and sandwiches on a bench and perched on it.

Dad switched off his lathe and wiped his enormous hands down his leather apron. 'I was getting a bit peckish. Thanks, Alex.'

We munched in silence for a bit then I asked him, sort of, about the invisible cat.

'I was thinking about invisibility. . .'

'As you do.'

I ignored him. The whole family thought my passion for fantasy was hilarious. 'Is there any reason why eyes can't be invisible if the rest of you is?'

'That's a sensible question,' Dad said.

'Is it?' It wasn't often I was called sensible. Usually it was 'daydreamer' or, at school, 'easily distracted'.

Dad nodded. 'In order to see, light has to bounce off the retinas at the back of the eyes. If the retinas were invisible then light would pass through them and you wouldn't be able to see.'

That was interesting.

'What's brought this on?' Dad asked.

I shrugged. 'It's a new fantasy book I was reading, about being invisible. It got me thinking.'

'That can't be bad,' Dad said. He put his empty mug on the tray. 'Back to work – things to do.'

I could take a hint. I took the tray back to the kitchen. I decided to stock up on more cake and then go to the library on the other side of town and look up invisibility. It was a long walk. I needed energy reserves.

'No!' I stared in shock. The cake lay smashed on the floor. All the buttercream had been licked off and jammy red paw prints led to the hallway.

'Cesare!' I yelled.

He was nowhere to be seen. I went to look for him.

Chapter Three
MIRROR, MIRROR

I searched every room on the three floors of the house and didn't find Cesare. That meant I had to try the boys' rooms. They each had a bedroom in the attic, one at either end, and the space in between was their studio. They still grumbled about it being way too small, and way too far from London, but they couldn't afford to live there.

I knocked on the door. 'Can I come in?'

'OK,' Sam's voice called. 'You can tell me what you think.'

That was a surprise. Usually Ben and Sam liked to keep their work private till it was ready to show. I opened the door, feeling honoured, and stared at the structure rearing halfway up to the ceiling. It was hung with mirrors turning at different speeds, capturing the light and splintering reflections

into hundreds of pieces. Sam was up a stepladder, adjusting the mirrors.

It was pretty spectacular even though it was only a small-scale version of the proper thing going up in Franklin's. I usually didn't encourage the boys – they were big-headed enough already – but this time I couldn't help saying, 'Wow!'

Sam jumped down, his daft grin appearing in flashes of mirror as he dropped to the floor.

'You like?'

'Yes. What's it called?'

'The Perception of Imperceptible Things,' Sam said, adjusting one of the mirrors.

'I have no idea what that means. I still like it. Is the real installation exactly like this?'

Sam's loopy grin got wider. The boys' art might be weird but their enthusiasm always made you look twice.

'The artwork proper's a lot bigger and more spectacular. We've had a delay with the scaffolding.' Sam shook his head in exasperation. 'Ben's sorting it now. As soon as it's done we're going to add more to the framework – extra mirrors, lights and. . . other things.'

I knew better than to ask what they were. Sometimes the 'other things' scared even me.

They did an installation on war once that gave me nightmares for a week.

'What sort of lights?' I asked.

'Fairy lights.'

'You're kidding!'

'Course I am. We're using neon. And holograms.'

Sam's grin faded and his eyes sort of unfocussed, which meant he was seeing stuff in his mind's eye.

He blinked and re-focussed. 'Were you being nosey or did you want something?'

'Charming. I'm looking for Cesare,' I said. 'He knocked one of Mum's cakes on the floor and ate all the buttercream. He'll probably be sick.'

'I haven't seen him.' Sam was serious for once. The boys kept Cesare out of the studio in case he spoiled their work. Not so much the installations as the drawings and paintings they did at the planning stage. Cesare could really damage them, like he did my chewed-up homework.

Just at that moment one of the spinning mirrors reflected Cesare sneaking out through the door. The mirror twirled again and the reflection was gone.

I blinked. There was definitely no cat. It must've been a shadow captured for a second in the glass.

'I'm going to clear up the mess in the kitchen before Mum gets back,' I said. 'You coming down for lunch?'

'May as well.'

Downstairs I cleaned up the cake while Sam helped himself to half the contents of the fridge. There was still no sign of Cesare.

I left Sam pigging out and went to the local library. Like everything else in Golden Bay it was really, really old-fashioned. Outside it looked like a Gothic castle, all turrets and battlements, and inside it looked like Dracula's study. The bays of books were heavy, dark wood with white marble statues of famous writers teetering on the tops. In between the bays were polished wooden tables and chairs with legs as thick as an elephant's ankles. You practically needed a forklift truck to move them.

Amazingly for Golden Bay there was a computerised library system but, even better, there were loads of books. Reading was my thing; I'd die if I couldn't read. This time though I wasn't after my favourite fantasy titles; I was going to do some research.

The librarian helped me find material on optics. It didn't mention invisibility in any of them.

I went to try an online search. The terminal had a sign saying: SYSTEM DOWN. Typical.

I gave up my search for invisibility information and chose more fantasy fiction instead. I sat on the floor, my back against a bookcase, and read.

It was only when a smiley young library assistant nudged my foot and said, 'We're closing in a bit,' that I remembered to check the time. Six thirty! Dinner was at seven.

I took out a couple of books and ran home.

Cesare and I arrived at the same time, just as Mum was dishing up the dinner. He was mewing pitifully as if we hadn't fed him for days. Mum did manage to restrain herself from feeding him till the humans had finished eating, but the minute the meal was over she filled his dish.

I took our plates to the dishwasher. When I turned round, Cesare's bowl was empty and he was meowing mournfully for more.

'That was quick, even for you,' I said ignoring the sad face and the winsome winding round my ankles.

'Think again, pussycat. You've already had half a kilo of buttercream today. You'll explode if you have more food.'

Mum picked him up and cooed at him. He purred loudly, closed his eyes and rubbed his head under Mum's chin. She fell for it.

'Give him some biscuits, Alex,' she said.

She was so gullible.

'I'm not clearing up if he's sick,' I said firmly as I poured the snacks into his bowl.

Mum put Cesare down and he strolled over to the dish, sniffed the biscuits, sat down and stared at them in disdain.

'Mr Picky,' I said. 'You're not getting anything else.'

Cesare glared at me. I ignored him and went back to the dishwasher.

To my surprise, when I turned round a moment later, the biscuits had gone.

★

A monster wind blew up that night. It churned the sea into giant waves that hurtled over the surface and squirted huge jets of foam into the air. Outside my rattling window, trees thrashed, the wind moaning and roaring in their branches. I drew the curtains and they swayed in the wind leaking through the window.

The catch on my bedroom door clicked, the door floated open and Cesare strolled in.

I turfed him out. He gave me one of his evil looks.

'You know you're not allowed in the bedrooms,' I said. 'Go away.'

Cesare sat down.

'Please yourself.' I shut the door properly and went back to bed with a book. I read a few chapters till the wind died down to a soothing moan. I yawned, closed the book, switched the light out and burrowed deep under the duvet. I went straight to sleep.

In the night I half-woke to feel Cesare's feet coming up the bed towards me. He snuggled up against my back and purred loudly.

Already drifting off, I mumbled crossly, 'Make yourself comfy, why don't you?' and went back to sleep.

As soon as I woke in the morning I remembered the cat. There was a warm patch where he'd been sleeping but no sign of him. He knew he was in disgrace for sneaking back into the room and was in hiding. I looked under the bed and behind the curtains. Nothing.

I flopped back on the bed, puzzled. How had Cesare got in? I knew for sure I'd closed the door properly. I jumped up and opened it. Cesare was curled up outside.

I goggled at him.

Had I dreamt the whole thing? I'd just decided I must have when I felt a furry body brush past my ankles. I looked down. There was nothing there.

Cesare uncurled with a happy little mewling sound and licked an empty space in front of him. The empty space began to purr loudly and two large, slanted yellow eyes stared at me out of nowhere.

I sagged against the doorframe for support. The invisible cat had followed me home.

Chapter Four
PAWS 4 THOUGHT

I clicked encouragingly at the cats and they trotted back into my bedroom mewing for food. Now what? I thought. I didn't want a magic cat. I'd learned the hard way that magic comes back on you. This cat was going to have to go.

Cesare and his new friend were getting impatient. They wanted their breakfast so I stopped panicking, shut them in my bathroom and ran down to the kitchen for supplies.

How could I have been so dim? Missing all the obvious signs yesterday: the dog barking madly at an unseen thing on the wall; the way Cesare's food disappeared so quickly after he'd refused it; the way the invisicat had sneaked into my room and slept on my bed all night after I'd locked Cesare out.

I gathered up cat food and a couple of spare bowls from the utility room and hurtled upstairs.

I plonked the bowls on the bathroom floor and filled them with food and water. While the cats were troughing, another thought flashed through my brain.

I dashed downstairs again, grabbed a bag of cat litter, a scoop and a spare tray from the utility room and hauled them back upstairs. I sorted the litter tray in the bathroom.

When they'd finished eating, I let the cats curl up on my bed while I thought about the invisicat. Maybe the cat that had appeared in the installation mirror the day before wasn't Cesare at all. It had seemed pretty large and Cesare was still a kitten.

I got a hand mirror and held it up to the purr that was all I could detect of the invisicat. There it was in the glass; grey and fluffy, like a very large version of Cesare but with a less grumpy face. I wondered if the cats were related. They were definitely very happy with each other, grooming away and purring like small engines.

I hurled myself back against my pillows and groaned. What was I going to do now?

By rights I should take the cat back to *Paws 4 Thought.* It did belong to the pet shop man. Or maybe it didn't. Maybe he'd stolen it. There was no way of knowing.

Whatever, I didn't fancy facing up to the man in the pet shop. He'd been bad-tempered the day before, and he'd probably be worse if I told him I'd accidentally lured his special cat away. This wasn't getting any easier.

I could hardly let the invisicat roam around free. It was firm friends with Cesare now and the pair of them working as a team could probably reduce the house to rubble. I shuddered and thought for a nanosecond about telling my family. No. None of them would believe me; they'd say it was another of my fantasies. And even if they did believe me, they'd make me take the cat back to *Paws 4 Thought*. Either that or they'd send it to some research place to be experimented on while the scientists tried to find out what made it invisible. I couldn't let either of those things happen.

I'd have to decide quickly; I could hear noises of people moving about. Mum was going to take more cakes to Charles before coming back to bake for the installation preview the next day. Dad was going to do some final adjustments to fitments and even the boys were getting up early to go to Franklin's to tweak the installation.

The only thing I could do was lock the cats in for the time being and hope a brilliant idea would

light up my brain sooner or later and solve the problem of having an invisible cat in the house.

'Come on, cats.' They followed me trustingly into the bathroom and I piled up the food bowl again. As soon as they dived in to eat I ran out of my bedroom, closed the door, very firmly, and went down for breakfast.

My family were finalising arrangements for the day. I got assigned to general duties helping out Mum, which was what I expected.

I grabbed my jacket and heard a rattling noise. It was the box of treats. The toy was in my other pocket. When the pet shop man threw me out the day before it had happened so quickly I'd left without paying.

That was useful. It gave me a perfect excuse to go back to *Paws 4 Thought*. Maybe that would help me decide what to do next.

★

Mum and I used the lift up to the Terrace Restaurant to give Charles his cakes. I still didn't raise my eyes to look at the liftman; I kept them trained on his shoes. They were very shiny. He didn't speak except to ask where we wanted to go and announce when we'd arrived.

Even with Mum there it was still a relief to get out of the lift. I'd had quite enough of magic with the invisicat. I didn't want to risk accidentally getting involved in any more by speaking to the liftman.

Mum stayed to talk business to Charles while I went to *Paws 4 Thought* to pay for the treats and the toy. I told Mum what I was doing.

'Don't be long,' she said.

I promised and used the stairs to get to the lobby. There was still a lot of hammering going on behind the shrouded installation. There were also raised voices. I wasn't sure if Ben and Sam were shouting to each other or at the scaffolders. The boys got intense when it came to their art.

There was no sign of the pet shop man in *Paws 4 Thought*. I was about to ping a brass bell on the counter when I saw a stack of business cards next to it. I picked one up. It read:

PAWS 4 THOUGHT

Bartholomew Magus
Licensed supplier of
small animals, fish and birds
Caters for all your pet's needs
FRANKLIN'S EMPORIUM - Unit 10
Ground Floor

I put it in my pocket and dinged the bell.

'I'll be out in a minute,' a voice called from behind a dark curtain at the back of the shop.

I took the chance to check out the animals. The fish were the same as the day before. I went into the rodents section. Yesterday there had been two chinchillas. Now there was only one. Must've sold the other, I thought. That was heartless; chinchillas are very sociable. I bent down to talk to the lonely animal. Four eyes stared back at me. Four eyes? Another invisible creature.

I went from cage to cage and in all of them there was a least one invisible animal. Pairs of confused eyes blinked from the back of the cages. That was bad enough, but the birds were worse. There was a parrot that was only a muted squawk and two beady black eyes that glared accusingly at me. And there was a single lovebird snuggling up to nothing. I only knew another bird was there because I could see them both reflected in their little mirror, the invisible one with its eyes closed.

I went round a second time and noticed some of the visible animals were a bit faded, not exactly transparent but sort of. . . weirdly insubstantial.

I had no idea why Mr Magus was turning the animals invisible but I did know he was making them all miserable. I made up my mind.

'I can't help you,' I said to the parrot, 'but I'm not bringing the invisible cat back.'

'You've got my cat?'

Mr Magus had sneaked up on me from behind the curtain.

I stared dumbly. It was impossible to pretend I hadn't said it.

Mr Magus gave a half-snarl, half-sneer. 'Bring that cat back.'

'Why?'

'Because it's mine. And because I can use it to help complete my experiments.'

That made me surer than ever that I wasn't going to let him have the invisicat. I started to back away.

He thrust his hand into his sagging black velvet pocket, drew it out again and threw a handful of glittering dust all over me. It settled for an instant then evaporated – poof!

Mr Magus began to chant softly in a strange language. My head swam. I made unsteadily for the door and came face to face with Mum.

'You're still here then,' she said. 'Have you paid yet?'

Mr Magus stopped chanting and sneered, 'She hasn't, but she will, oh yes, she will.'

'You needn't make a song and dance about it, it was a mistake,' Mum said sharply. 'Pay the man, Alex.'

I paid Mr Magus and Mum propelled me out of the shop.

'Steer clear of him in future,' she said.

She didn't need to tell me that – he'd creeped me out, big time. He was much, much worse than the liftman.

Chapter Five
FADING AWAY

At home Mum said. 'You're a bit peaky. Are you feeling all right?'

'I'm a bit tired,' I admitted. It was true. I thought it was probably all the running up and down stairs I'd done.

Mum gave me a hug. 'Go and have an hour or two's rest then see how you feel.'

That sounded ok to me. Any excuse to read.

Mum went off to her chef's kitchen to get started on a marathon bake for the exhibition preview. She'd wanted to do a miniature version of the installation in cake. The boys wanted to keep it secret and wouldn't let her. I didn't blame them.

I went into my room carefully, making sure the cats didn't escape. I needn't have worried; they

were curled up together on my bed. Cesare seemed to be fast asleep with his chin in the air and his nose pointing upwards. It was eerie even though I knew he was resting his head on the invisicat. That was the only way I did know it was there as its eyes were closed. They opened as I came in and it mewed. That alerted Cesare and both cats bounded off the bed and pleaded for food.

'Give me a chance,' I said, trying to wade through two cats winding impatiently round and round my ankles.

I gave them some biscuits, kicked off my shoes, lay on my bed and picked up my book. I'd got to a part where the main character, who had stowed away on an airship, had been discovered by the captain. I read on. The cats came and curled up next to me. The stowaway fought the captain tooth and nail, up and down the ship. He grabbed at her, she slipped over the side of the ship and was hurtling through the clouds when there was a knock at the door and Mum's voice said, 'Can I come in?'

Why now? I thought savagely.

'Just a minute.'

I pinned a startled cat under each arm, dashed to the bathroom, dropped them and closed the door.

I hopped back onto the bed. 'Come in.'

Mum sat on the end of my bed.

'You really do look a bit pale.' She took my book and put it on the bedside table. 'Stop reading and have a nap.'

A nap? How old did she think I was? Three?

I gave a pretend yawn. 'OK.' As soon as she'd gone I was going to open that book again. I was desperate to know what happened to the character plummeting to Earth.

There was a clawing at the bathroom door and angry meowing.

'What's that?' Mum opened the bathroom door and Cesare shot out, ran through the bedroom and disappeared onto the landing.

It was a good job he moved fast. The invisicat's eyes followed him at the same speed and Mum didn't notice them.

So much for my plotting, I thought. I might just as well have let them out in the first place.

'What was he doing in the bathroom?' Mum asked.

'No idea,' I fibbed.

She shook her head in exasperation and went.

That was a narrow escape, which was good. But now I had the problem of finding

the invisicat yet again and putting it where it couldn't be found while I worked out what to do with it.

In the meantime I thought I'd better bag up the leftovers in the cats' bowls and the drek in the litter tray. Mum hadn't had time to notice it but she would if she came back and smelled a pong. Then I'd have to admit to locking Cesare in the bathroom without being able to say why. The book would have to wait.

I filled a pedal bin liner and went to wash my hands before I took it down to the wheelie bin. As I rinsed off the soap, and the water sluiced over them, I thought my hands looked a bit peculiar. The skin was almost transparent and I could see my veins and sinews underneath.

Queasiness flooded through me and I sat on the edge of the bath. Tentatively I held out my hands. I wasn't mistaken. My skin was definitely transparent. I rolled up my jeans and examined my ankles and feet. They were transparent too. In fact, they were even more transparent. I could see bones.

No wonder Mum thought I looked washed out. I was washed out. It was horrible. I was half way to becoming invisible.

Now I knew what Bartholomew Magus had been up to when he threw sparkly dust at me and started chanting. He'd cast a spell on me. Why hadn't I made the connection before? Because the spell had made me feel light-headed and unable to think straight.

On the good side, Mum had interrupted Magus before he could complete the spell. That explained the semi-invisibility but even though I was only faded, I'd still have to get the spell reversed. Being see-through was as bad as being invisible.

There was only one thing for it; the thing I'd been avoiding ever since I came back to Golden Bay with my family. I'd have to talk to the liftman. I needed to ask for his help.

'Nooo!' I drummed the side of the bath with my heels in frustration.

Magic was a dangerous business – it could go wrong and if it did, I just knew I'd end up in a worse state than I already was. I'd have to be very, very careful.

★

I covered myself up as much as I could. I pulled on a hoodie and rolled my sleeves down, crept

out of my room and sneaked quietly through the front door. Once I was outside I tucked my hands into my armpits and hurried through the back streets to the Emporium.

Franklin's was busy and it was easy to slip through the lobby without attracting attention. I waited in a corner by the lift and watched it go up and down, letting people out and taking them in. At last a man got out and no one got in. I rushed inside.

'Close the doors!'

The liftman pulled the iron grid across the door and pressed the 'close' button. The doors slid shut.

I pulled my hoodie back and held out my transparent hands.

'I need your help,' I told the liftman.

'I thought you might,' he said.

Chapter Six
THE POLTERGEIST

While I'd been waiting I'd had plenty of time to plan what I was going to say to the liftman. The rules of his magic were very simple, even if they did have a habit of going wrong. I had to ask for something and make a wish – and the wish had to be in rhyme.

I was feeling embarrassed. The liftman must've known I'd spent weeks trying to avoid him yet now I was going to ask him a big favour. I realised I was staring at his shoes again. I flipped my hood back and made myself make eye contact. It was only polite.

'I want you to work some magic for me.'

'I see.'

'Bartholomew Magus cast a spell to make me invisible. He was interrupted and it's only half-worked.'

I lifted a hand again. In the light of the lift lamps it looked like a cloudy, full-colour x-ray.

'Can you reverse the spell that did this?'

The liftman was silent, patient as an ancient rock on the beach. He nodded.

All right, I thought, here we go. I crossed my fingers behind my back and hoped I'd got everything covered.

'I wish to be just like before

So free me from this evil curse.

Make me visible once more

And please, this wicked spell reverse.'

The lift abruptly shot up a floor and stopped. Even though I knew the new spell wasn't going to work immediately, I couldn't help wondering how long it would take for me to get back to normal. When I had needed a spell undone last summer, it had taken the time it took to walk down the stairs to the ground floor to take effect.

I pulled my hood up. 'Thank you,' I said.

The old man's sharp eyes peered from under his beetling white eyebrows. 'Are you sure there is nothing else you wish to ask for?'

I didn't like the sound of that. 'Yes, I'm positive,' I said.

'Then perhaps one day I may ask a favour of you.'

I didn't like the sound of that either. From what I'd read, magicians had a habit of asking really difficult favours that got you into lots of trouble. You should never be beholden to a wizard.

'Maybe,' I said cautiously.

The liftman opened the grille and the doors. I kept my head down and wove my way through the shoppers to the stairs. I walked down them slowly to give the magic plenty of time to work. Sure enough, when I went back into the foyer and held out my hands they were solid again.

I practically skipped across the lobby, glad to be back to normal. ''Scuse me,' I said to a man standing in the doorway.

He didn't move. I stepped to one side and he glided in front of me. It was Bartholomew Magus and he was scowling.

Although I knew he wouldn't risk performing magic in public I wasn't going to hang around, just in case. I saw a gap in the steady trickle of customers leaving and dashed into it. In moments I was outside, skimming down the marble steps and onto the promenade.

I looked over my shoulder and saw Magus standing on the steps, watching me. I ran faster

than ever, making sure I went home by the network of twisting, back streets. Magus didn't follow me, which was a relief.

I went through the door in the wall round our garden, closed it and leaned back. I basked in the sun and got my breath back. A blackbird perched on top of Dad's workshop and sang. It was peaceful and serene.

Crash!

A huge smashing noise came from Dad's workshop. I dashed inside and found him standing bemused, a pile of plates and goblets on the floor underneath a shelf. Good job they were made of wood and not china.

'What happened?'

'I'm not sure,' Dad said. 'I think we've got a poltergeist.'

'A poltergeist!'

'A ghost that throws things.'

'Thanks, Dad. I've read enough ghost stories to know what a poltergeist is. They're not real.'

I started picking up the things on the floor.

'What really happened?'

Dad joined me. We put the plates and goblets on a bench near his lathe. 'I was carrying some stuff to the shelf when I heard Cesare mewing.

I didn't want him doing any damage and I made shooing noises. Then. . .'

Dad paused as if he couldn't quite believe what he'd seen. He scratched his head.

'One by one, all the things on the shelf fell off. It was exactly like they were being pushed off, except there wasn't anything there to push them. It must've been a poltergeist. My workshop is haunted!'

Dad was only half-joking. He didn't believe in ghosts any more than I did but he had no idea what else it could've been.

I knew. It was the invisicat. It must have wandered out of the house and down the garden into Dad's workshop, jumped on the shelf, mewed and been frightened when Dad made shooing noises. It had panicked and run along the shelf, knocking all Dad's precious work onto the floor.

'I bet it was Cesare,' I said heartily. 'He moves like greased lightning. You didn't see him, that's all.'

'You're humouring me,' Dad said. 'I know what I saw – or didn't see.'

At that moment Cesare sauntered in and leapt lithely onto the bench. He regarded Dad insolently.

'You're asking for trouble,' Dad said, glaring at the cat.

Appearing tentatively round the door came two floaty yellow eyes.

I wasn't going to let the invisicat make more mischief. It was going back to my room.

I scooped Cesare up. 'I'll take him to the house before he causes any more damage.'

'It wasn't Cesare,' Dad insisted.

I stroked the cat's head. 'Come on kitty,' I cooed, trying to imitate Mum's soppy cat voice. 'Let's go and find your treats.'

I left as quickly as possible hoping that the eyes would follow Cesare and me. They did.

Mum was still in her kitchen and I had no bother getting upstairs without being seen.

Cesare writhed and tried to escape. I got scratched – a lot – but I held onto him until we were safely in my room. I washed my scratches and then gave the cats yet more snacks.

While they were occupied I settled back on my bed with my book. I got so absorbed I hardly noticed the cats glide on to the bed and cuddle up next to me. I did notice when Cesare started scratching himself vigorously and, from the way the bed was vibrating, so did the invisicat. I hoped

it didn't have fleas. I wondered if fleas would be visible if they jumped off the invisicat. And disappear again when they burrowed into its fur.

Another thought trampled over the others: I should've asked the liftman to make the invisicat visible as well as me.

Maybe that's what he meant when he asked if I wanted to make another wish. But how could he know about the invisicat? I was certain I hadn't told him.

It was no good going back to Franklin's on my own now that Bartholomew Magus was watching for me, so I couldn't take the invisicat to the liftman.

There was no point in worrying. I couldn't do anything. I paid attention to my book instead and the cats stopped scratching and purred themselves to sleep.

I finished my book at the same moment my stomach started to tell me it was empty and Dad banged on the door.

'Mum says dinner's ready!' he boomed and his footsteps plonked off down the landing.

The cats woke with a start and went berserk. They ran round the bedroom, up the curtains, into the bathroom.

Smash! Smash!

Soap and tooth mugs went flying, bathmats went skidding over the floor, talc got knocked over and fell in a cloud over the invisicat. It instantly became visible, in a spectral sort of way: ghostly white with a pair of startled, glowing yellow eyes.

The two animals stopped dead in surprise. Cesare tentatively offered his nose and the cats sniffed each other. The talc went up their noses and they sneezed.

Panic set in again. The cats screeched, shot into the air and launched themselves like small furry battering rams at the door. It flew open. The cats hurtled onto the landing and torpedoed towards the stairs. From halfway down I heard Dad bellow something really rude.

Poor Dad. I knew he was going to have a hard time trying to convince everyone that he'd seen a poltergeist *and* a ghost cat. I was right.

Chapter Seven
THE SEVEN MYSTERIES OF GOLDEN BAY

'Really, Peter,' Mum said, helping herself to a heap of salad, 'first you see a poltergeist and now you see a ghost cat. Are you sure it wasn't Cesare?'

Dad gloomily ladled a second helping of risotto onto his plate.

'I didn't see the poltergeist – they're invisible by nature. This ghost cat was just that – a cat that's a ghost. It was a transparent white with giant yellow eyes. And it wasn't Cesare because he was chasing it.'

Ben and Sam were too busy eating to make fun of Dad. They just smirked at each other and raised their eyebrows.

I kept my head down and ate. I was worried. If the invisicat was anything like Cesare it was going to be attracted by the smell of food. Food was a cat magnet. I surreptitiously glanced round the kitchen. To my horror Cesare was entering the room closely followed by the familiar floaty eyes. The thin film of talc had gone. Cesare and the invisicat must've groomed it away.

The eyes assessed the height of a big old kitchen dresser where Mum had laid pudding out. There was lots of cream.

The invisicat sprang. It couldn't get a grip on the polished surface, skidded right across the top and flew off the other end. On the way it knocked off the pudding, the dishes and the spoons. Everyone span round and stared as, one by one, things cascaded to the floor.

The invisicat yowled, ran for the cat flap and burst through with Cesare close behind.

There was silence for a moment.

'I told you there was a poltergeist,' Dad said smugly.

★

We were all unusually quiet that night. The boys went up to their studio and Mum put the finishing

touches to the food for the grand preview. I was roped in to help her and so was Dad. He was the only cheerful one. He was happy to be vindicated over the poltergeist and whistled as he helped Mum.

Afterwards I tried to find the cats. There were in hiding and I gave up. At least, I thought, if they do anything awful now it won't come back on me.

I left the cat flap unlocked and went up to bed. Before I started reading, I made up a rhyme to chant to the liftman next day. I was going to talk to him while my family was in Franklin's. I wanted to ask him to make the invisicat, and the other pets in *Paws 4 Thought*, return to normal. The rhyme had been harder to make up than usual and had Latin in it. I felt pleased with myself after I double-checked the spelling and the meaning. It was perfect.

I settled cosily in bed, finished my book and started on the next one in the series. I read about halfway, to where the mechanisms for keeping airships aloft broke down and they all sank, quicker and quicker, through the clouds.

It seemed a good place to stop and I went to sleep dreaming of airships manned by invisible cats with ginormous yellow eyes.

★

The next morning Mum and Dad had everything ready for the preview but since it wasn't due to open until four in the afternoon they weren't going to set up the catering things until one. I wanted to check on the pet shop animals but I still felt uneasy about Magus – he was definitely after me. I decided to wait until the afternoon, so that I could go to Franklin's with my parents, and spend the morning doing more research at the library. If the Emporium had a history of magic, I might learn something to help me avoid making mistakes when I spoke to the liftman again.

I did look for the cats first but there was still no sign of them. I was at the library when it opened at ten. I was first in.

'You're keen,' the librarian said.

'I want to find out about the history of Franklin's Emporium,' I told him. 'Right from the beginning.'

'Ok.' He led me to a section labelled 'Local History'. A marble bust with 'HERODOTUS' chiselled round the plinth stared down sternly from blank white eyes.

The librarian piled huge leather books on the table and put two pamphlets next to them. One

was old and speckly. The other looked newer, though not that new, and had an unusual cover.

'These leaflets are the only documentation we've got. They're quite basic,' he said and grinned. 'They were a secretive lot, the Franklins, even when the Emporium was at its most famous. You'll probably get more information from these.'

He nodded toward the massive leather books. They were bound copies of the local newspaper, *The Golden Bay Bugle.*

'If you read this,' he tapped the newer pamphlet, 'and find any interesting events, you can check them against the newspapers to see if there's more information there. Anything else you want to know, come and ask me.'

I said thanks and picked up the old, blotchy pamphlet.

It showed the grand opening of Franklin's and had a picture of the founder, Eli Franklin. I thought he might look like the liftman, and scrutinised his face carefully. I couldn't see a resemblance.

Inside there were more pictures: the mayor in his robes; the right honourable someone or other cutting a ribbon stretched across the front entrance and old adverts for all sorts of things to buy in Franklin's. They sounded very expensive. There

were descriptions like: 'sewn from the finest silk' and 'diamonds by Tiffany's'.

I looked at the second booklet. It was fatter than the first one and classy. The white cover had a blue border like the one running round the entrance to the store. Across the front it said:

FRANKLIN'S EMPORIUM

1925 – 1956

I opened it.

It said the building went up in 1925 in the latest art deco style. It belonged to old Mr Eli Franklin. There was the same picture of him as the one in the other pamphlet. The Emporium was opened by Edward, Prince of Wales. There was a picture of him too.

After the opening, other royal people, and even film stars of the time, stayed in Golden Bay and shopped at Franklin's. There were lots of pictures of them.

I skipped through most of the rest until I got to the end.

The last thing the pamphlet said was that there'd been a dispute between the two sons who had inherited the store when old Eli died

in 1932. The elder son, Arthur, didn't want to sell the Emporium but the younger son, Walter did. Walter won and the store was eventually sold. It went out of fashion, fell into disrepair and closed down. There were no pictures of Arthur or Walter.

It was interesting there was no mention of magic.

I picked up one of the massive books, *The Golden Bay Bugle – 1932*. It was like lifting a paving slab. The newspapers were yellowed and crinkly. The pages smelled musty and rustled loudly when I turned them.

The report on Arthur and Walter's fight was front-page news.

'FRANKLIN BROS COME TO BLOWS DURING BOARD MEETING!' the headline yelled above a photograph of the Emporium.

'Police were called to Franklin's Emporium yesterday after a board meeting descended into a tempestuous bout of fisticuffs between the two senior partners, Mr Arthur Franklin and Mr Walter Franklin.

Mr Walter Franklin had eloquently persuaded the other board members to vote in accordance with his wish to sell the Emporium. Mr Arthur Franklin took such violent exception to this decision that he flung himself

upon his defenceless brother, eventually pinioning him to the boardroom table.

So fierce had the pugilism become that another board member summoned the police whilst several others were obliged to wrest Mr Arthur Franklin from the hapless form of his brother.

Once Mr Walter Franklin had regained his breath and composure, he ordered his brother to leave the premises before the arrival of the constabulary. Nothing has been seen of him since.'

There was still nothing about magic. I read a bit further on and found out that Walter soon disappeared with his share of the money from the sale of Franklin's. Neither brother was ever seen again.

I closed the book with a thud that made the table shake and slumped forward, my head on the leather cover.

'Have you gone to sleep or are you in despair?' It was the librarian.

'In despair. I didn't find what I was looking for.'

'Which was?'

I hesitated. Even though librarians were great and always found you what you wanted, I wasn't sure about mentioning magic. I decided to go for it.

'I heard that Franklin's Emporium might be a magic sort of place but these,' I nodded at the pamphlets and newspapers, 'don't mention magical things. I guess I was wrong.'

'Ah ha! Don't give up so easily.' The librarian plucked a book off the shelf behind me. 'This is called 'The Seven Mysteries of Golden Bay.'

He flicked through the pages. 'Now where is it? Yep, here we go: Chapter Two – The Strange Disappearance of Arthur Franklin.'

'Have a go at that.' He gave me the book and went off with that smile of satisfaction librarians have when they find you what you want.

I smoothed the book flat on the table and began to read.

Chapter Eight THE MAGICIANS' BATTLE

I was right; the book said that Arthur and Walter had both become involved in magic after touring the world as young men. Walter was interested in the magic of darkness and Arthur in the magic of light.

After their father died, the brothers discovered that old Eli, knowing Arthur and Walter were at daggers drawn, had divided shares in Franklin's Emporium between several family members as well as his sons. The brothers quarrelled. Arthur wanted to keep the store; Walter wanted to sell up and take the money.

As the quarrel grew worse, Walter used dark magic to make the other shareholders vote with him.

When Arthur realised what Walter had done, he challenged him to a magicians' duel. That was what the fight in the boardroom really was. The author of the book had got the true story from a waiter who was serving the board members at the meeting.

I could just imagine it. I closed my eyes and ran it through my mind's eye like a film.

Arthur pushes back his chair and stands. Every face turns in his direction but he only has eyes for his brother.

'I can't allow you to sell the Emporium and squander our inheritance.'

Walter sneers. 'You can't stop me.' He lifts his arm and indicates the other board members. 'I have their support.'

Arthur nods. 'I know. Therefore, I challenge you to a duel and the prize is Franklin's Emporium.'

Without warning, Arthur throws a stream of blue light at his brother. Walter dodges and counter-attacks with a bolt of red light.

The board members leap to their feet, knocking over chairs in their haste to get away. A waiter, who's been standing quietly in the background, is pushed over. He scrambles under the table for protection from the sizzling light hurtling back and forth across the room, tearing

curtains, zapping books from the shelves, knocking down clocks, ornaments, bottles of wine and crystal glasses.

Arthur weaves a cage of light round himself. Walter retaliates with a cage of shadows. Both men levitate. They sway in the air for a moment then start to circle each other.

Round and round they go, up and down, faster and faster until they are little more than a shining and a murky blur. Arthur throws out strands of light like ropes and tightens them, bit by bit, round Walter's protective cage. Walter cries out. Arthur gives a last pull and the shadows fracture and break up. Walter falls to the floor by the table.

Arthur hovers triumphantly over his brother and begins to entwine him in a tight cocoon of light. Walter scrabbles one hand free, stretches it out and grabs at the waiter who is cowering under the table.

'Free me, brother, unless you want harm to come to this boy!' Walter shouts.

Arthur hesitates.

Walter tightens his grip and the young man cries out, 'Help me!'

Arthur's hand drops to his side and the skein of light around Walter fades, disappears.

Walter stands up, the waiter still in his grip. 'You're a weak fool, Arthur. You had me in your

power and yet you let me go to save this insignificant underling.'

'Any of Franklin's employees are more important than the business,' Arthur says.

Walter shakes his head in disbelief. 'Kneel,' he commands.

Arthur kneels and his brother conjures up shadows. When Arthur is completely enveloped in darkness, Walter shoves the waiter away and holds both arms out, palms upwards. He begins to mould the shadows into a ball, squeezes it tighter and tighter until it's the size of an egg.

With a cry of triumph, he throws the ball into the air and it vanishes.

Walter turns to the waiter. 'That's the last we'll see of him.'

The waiter flees.

And that was where the story ended. I opened my eyes.

One of the Franklin brothers had to be the old liftman – he knew everything about the store – but which one? I didn't even have a photograph or illustration to help me decide.

I took the book to the counter. The librarian was there, helping the library assistants deal with a queue of readers.

'Any use?' he asked, waving the bar scanner over the book.

'Yes and no,' I said. 'There are gaps.'

'Keep looking and if there's anything else I can help with, let me know.'

'OK,' I said though I thought it was unlikely I'd get any more information from books in the library.

The sun had come out and so had the tourists. I wandered down to the beach and sat on a rock, watching the sea and the swimmers thrashing around in the cold water.

I thought about Arthur and Walter, the two magicians, and about the other magical people I'd met in Franklin's: Bartholomew Magus, and Harriette, who'd sold me magic gloves last summer. She'd changed from a little girl to an old lady and then to a young woman, all in a few hours. Where was Harriette now? Come to that, if one of the Franklin brothers *was* the liftman, where was the other one?

I threw a pebble into a rock pool and startled a small fish. It was time to go home for lunch and forget about the mystery of the liftman, for now.

Chapter Nine
THE INSTALLATION

With Mum and Dad around – as well as the boys and all the shoppers – I wasn't too worried about bumping into Bartholomew Magus. I even decided I'd go into *Paws 4 Thought* and double check on the animals before I went to the liftman and asked him to cast my spell.

First I helped Dad set up the tables. Mum had done a great job with the catering, and we set her cakes out on tablecloths decorated in blue and white patterns echoing the designs all round the huge entrance hall. As she hadn't been allowed to bake an installation cake she'd made a great big Franklin's Emporium one instead, surrounded by lots of cupcakes with images from all over the store.

I could hear the boys talking behind the red cloth covering the installation. I only caught snatches;

they were still worried that the scaffolders hadn't constructed the framework properly.

The VIPs started to arrive at half past three. The art critics were first, and the press, then the local bigwigs and the mayor, jingling his bling. The boys were called out for a photo opportunity.

Mum and Dad were transfixed and I took the chance to slip away to *Paws 4 Thought* while they were staring at the fuss being made of Ben and Sam. I checked cautiously. Bartholomew Magus wasn't there. Still, I had a shock when I went inside. Apart from the fish, all the animals had gone. The cage doors were open and there were no shadowy creatures or frightened little eyes inside.

I had a good look round and even reached into the cages in case any invisible animals were asleep, or worse. Still nothing.

'Where are you?' I said out loud.

'Here!' A bony hand gripped my arm and a pair of spiteful, pale blue eyes leaned towards me.

It was Bartholomew Magus, and he was invisible.

'Where are the animals?' I said.

I heard a sneering chuckle. 'As you can see, my experiments are complete. I had no further use

for those creatures. They can take their chances out in the world.'

That was cruel. They weren't used to looking out for themselves; they might not survive. I was so angry I kicked out hard without thinking. Crunch. My toe connected with his shin – or at least, it was the right height for his shin.

'Ow! Ow! Ow!' he squealed and let go of me. The blue eyes vanished – he'd squished them closed in agony.

There were a couple of soft thuds as he hopped away and then a crash as he collided with a pyramid of special offer tins of dog food.

I ran out hoping the tins rolling all over the floor would stop him getting to his feet quickly and coming after me.

The boys and the dignitaries were still posing for photos in front of the cloaked installation. Behind them I could see lots of little eyes heading for cover under the red cloth. The invisible animals were trying to hide.

I had to get to the lift immediately. Those animals were going to make a mess of my brothers' artwork; their reputations would be ruined and it'd be all over the press and social media. Mum and Dad were too absorbed watching the boys

being minor celebrities to notice me creeping fast round the edge of the lobby and heading for the lift.

I pressed the call button and hopped up and down. 'Come ON!' Why was it taking so long?

There was a ping, a rattle and the doors opened.

'About time.'

I dived into the lift and shot into a corner, puffing with relief. For once the liftman didn't look at me. His gaze was fixed on the open door. I glanced in the same direction and saw two baleful, pale blue eyes glaring right at me. They started to advance, swivelled towards the liftman, stopped, narrowed into angry slits and withdrew.

The doors closed. The liftman tilted his head enquiringly to one side.

'That was Bartholomew Magus. I didn't know he was going to be invisible,' I said. 'I just came to ask if you'd make his cat and all the pets he's made invisible go back to normal.'

'All of them. Hmm. That's strong magic indeed. Magus is almost as powerful a wizard as I am,' the liftman said.

It was the first time I'd heard him admit he was a magician.

'But you can do it?'

'Oh yes,' he said softly. 'Make your wish.'

I hoped it was going to work.

'I wish the creatures, beasts and birds,
Changed back to how they were before.
Please speak now your magic words
And the status quo restore.'

The lift went up like a rocket. My legs buckled and I found myself kneeling on the floor. The lift stopped as abruptly as it had started. I got up, knees aching.

The lift opened onto the terrace restaurant right at the top of the Emporium. I was going to have to run down seven flights of stairs.

The liftman quirked an eyebrow at me. 'Strong magic takes hard work.'

I flew down the steps and burst out into the lobby.

The mayor was pulling a cord round the installation and cameras were flashing. The red cloths slithered down and lay in a crimson puddle on the floor.

The crowd gasped, and so did I.

Chapter Ten
DISASTER!

The installation was a double helix of scaffolding, twisting its way upwards. Lasers played, neon flashed and glinting mirrors spun slowly, revealing the invisible animals and birds in the turning glass.

On the good side, everyone but me and the boys thought the reflections of the invisible creatures were part of the installation. People began clapping.

'How did they do that?' the mayor said.

'No idea,' a minion answered. 'Some techno thing I guess.'

Hah! Techno thing – it was magic, Bartholomew Magus's magic. Why hadn't the liftman's more powerful magic cancelled it out?

The lights on the wall, showing which floor the lift had got to, were winking their way downwards.

'Come on!' I muttered, fists clenched. The last light glowed red and the doors opened. The gasps of astonishment increased.

I turned back to the installation. Small furry animals were running up and down it and birds randomly perched everywhere.

'They're not a techno thing,' the mayor said.

The minion was speechless.

A woman suddenly let out a piercing scream and pointed towards me.

What had I done?

All eyes, including my family's, swung round to me. More screams and a lot of laughter, echoed round the lobby. My parents were elbowing their way towards me, furious expressions on their faces. My brothers were clutching each other, laughing.

I was mystified. I held out my hands, palms up, and shrugged. A shove in my back sent me staggering into the installation. I clung to the scaffolding, spun helplessly round and found myself facing Bartholomew Magus. And not just his eyes. The liftman's magic had worked on

him as well as the creatures and he was visible all right, too visible. Unlike the birds and animals, which were covered with fur or feathers, he only had skin. He'd had to take his clothes off to be completely invisible.

He snatched up a piece of the red cloth, wrapped it round himself and fled with a bunch of burly security guards in pursuit.

Mum and Dad reached me. 'Are you all right?' Mum asked.

I nodded and let go of the scaffolding. It wobbled. It creaked. It began, gradually, to fold in on itself.

'Run!' Dad shouted and grabbed my arm. Mum seized the other one and they propelled me away as the whole installation imploded. There were more screams and shouts, a volley of flashing camera lights and the thrumming of running feet.

Crash!

The installation lay in a heap in the middle of the lobby, debris puffing up and falling back. It creaked and moaned for a bit like a dying engine and then fell silent.

Quite a few people had fallen over and were being helped to their feet. The animals had all

run off and the birds were either flying round in circles or perching high in the ceiling.

'Is anyone hurt?' the mayor asked. Miraculously, nobody was. I checked out the lift. The doors were closing on the liftman, one hand raised in a protective gesture. He'd made some kind of shielding magic though how and why I had no idea.

Ben and Sam were standing by the ruins of their installation. I was amazed that they were cheerful. The famous critic they were talking to was smiling and making notes on a tablet. All three of them were acting animated and excited. Artists. I was never going to understand them.

The journalists and cameramen were having a great time too, dictating into their phones, tapping at tablets and taking pictures.

I helped Mum and Dad salvage what we could of the catering. The food was mostly squished or full of bits from the falling installation. The tables were fine and we soon had them stashed away in the unit. Mum was regretting having crockery and glasses instead of paper plates and plastic cups. The shards and slivers took a lot of sweeping away. Cleaners appeared from out of the blue, a bit like the security men. Mum said Franklin's

mysterious lawyers included cleaning and security in the package when she'd made the exhibition arrangements for the boys.

'Good job,' Dad said. 'I bet they didn't expect an exploding art exhibition. How's the insurance cover?'

I zoned out at that point. Mum was very sensible and I wasn't interested in insurance.

Franklin's was closed for the rest of the day while the clearing up went on. Several of the other unit owners moaned about it, though most understood.

We were exhausted by the time we were able to leave. Ben and Sam and a group of the VIPs, including the famous critic, had gone off for dinner.

'I'm not cooking tonight,' Mum said firmly.

'Nor me,' Dad said. 'We'll follow the boys' example and eat out.'

We went to *The Sole Provider*, the chippy down by the pier, and sat on benches, watching the tide play with the sea as we scoffed our fish and chips.

When we'd finished, we walked home through the dusk, arm in arm. As soon as we opened the front door Mum's hand flew to her mouth. 'Cesare – he hasn't eaten all day.'

'I think he'll survive,' Dad said.

'You can be so heartless, Peter,' Mum said.

'I know but you still love me.'

This was a routine I'd heard before. There would be kisses next.

'I'll feed him,' I said quickly and hurried to the kitchen. The cat flap had been left unlocked since Cesare and the invisicat shot through it the night before when I'd left out dry food and water. The cats had to have come back by now.

They had. They were curled up together on a cushioned chair. Cesare's pink tongue rasped rhythmically up and down the invisicat's grey fur and it paddled its paws contentedly against the cushion.

The liftman's magic *had* worked long-distance. The invisicat wasn't invisible any more.

'Mum, Dad,' I yelled, 'come and see this!'

'What's up?'

I dragged them over to the chair.

Mum's eyes widened and the soppy expression came over her face. 'It looks just like Cesare,' she said, stroking the invisicat.

'It might be his mother,' I said.

'We're not keeping it.' Dad frowned. 'I'll phone Cats' Protection.'

Mum picked up the invisicat who butted her gently under the chin.

'We'll see.'

I knew who was going to win this one.

Chapter Eleven
BROTHERS

The end of the holiday was chaotic. Ben and Sam had got glowing reviews of their installation with sympathetic accounts of the way it had collapsed. The reviews were so good that an agent took them on. She got a London gallery owner interested in exhibiting their work and found them studio space in an artists' cooperative. Ben and Sam were in a frenzy of packing and planning.

Mum and Dad spent most of their time in their units at Franklin's. They did a roaring last minute holiday trade with the tourists. I was happy to stay at home. Officially the boys were keeping an eye on me; unofficially, when I wasn't reading, I wandered round Golden Bay, exploring caves, watching the fishing boats in the harbour or parking myself at the library.

As long as I reported back regularly and let them know what I was doing, they were OK with it. And so was I.

The cats and I were the only calm ones in the house. Cesare was a reformed character. The invisicat was a soothing influence and the two of them adored each other. Dad wanted to call her Lucrezia, after Cesare Borgia's sister who went around poisoning people and having them assassinated. Mum said that wasn't the cat's nature at all and called her Angel. I thought Lucrezia was better but Mum got her way. The name stuck, and so did the cat.

The one thing I didn't do was go back to Franklin's Emporium. I wasn't scared. It was that I always seemed to end up in trouble there and I'd had enough of it. I held out until the last Friday morning of the holidays. It was wet and miserable. I didn't fancy the beach or the harbour so when Mum asked me to come and help her at *Fran's Fancies* I agreed. The bad weather made business slack and we had time to chat.

'What've you been doing with yourself this past week?' Mum asked me.

'Not much, chilling out, mostly.'

'Not reading? You're always reading.'

I'd been finishing off the other stories in The Seven Mysteries of Golden Bay and I'd brought the book with me. I took it out of my bag and opened it at Chapter Two.

'This tells you all about the Franklin brothers who inherited the Emporium from their father, Eli,' I told Mum. 'Arthur and Walter had a massive quarrel and a fight and disappeared in mysterious circumstances.'

'Did they?'

Mum took the book and flipped through it. 'No pictures,' she said disapprovingly. 'I'm like Alice – I don't think a book's much use without pictures.'

I wouldn't go that far. I liked my books big and fat with a lot of words going into complicated detail on the entire fantasy world I was reading about. But I did agree on one thing.

'A picture of Arthur and Walter would be helpful,' I said.

Mum gave me the book back. 'There might be one over there.' She pointed to the far end of the entrance hall. 'There's a whole collection of old photographs on that wall.'

'Really?' I crossed the lobby and scanned the black and white photographs. I'd never taken

any notice of them before; I'd thought they were part of the décor, not a record of Franklin's history.

Mum was right. In the middle of the display was a portrait of Eli and his family. I recognized him easily from his picture in the pamphlets. Next to him was his tired-looking wife, and in front, three small girls, posing stiffly in frilly dresses. At the back, one on either side of Eli and his wife, stood two tall, thin, dapper young men. Arthur and Walter.

I got up close and scrutinised the brothers. You couldn't tell from the faces which one dabbled in dark magic and which in light. They were very alike: angular and dark. Both men had thick, black hair. One of them had a pencil moustache. I studied it. Villains in old films usually had twirly moustaches. This one was too small to be twirled but it was definitely villainous-looking. It still didn't tell me if its owner was Arthur or Walter.

Without meaning to, I glanced over my shoulder at the lift as if the doors were going to open and reveal the answer. They were already open and the liftman was looking straight at me with sharp, inscrutable eyes.

I shivered and the doors slowly closed.
Walter, I thought.
Or maybe, Arthur?
I couldn't tell.

ACKNOWLEDGEMENTS

With thanks to Anthony Bradley for allowing me to describe his wonderful steampunk story as one of Alex's books.

Who's who in FRANKLIN'S EMPORIUM?

Each of the quotes below comes from one of the characters in the story. Match the character to what they say. Turn to the back of this section for the answers (no peeking!).

1. The old liftman
2. The librarian
3. Charles from Terrace Restaurant
4. Bartholomew Magus, the pet shop owner
5. Sam
6. Alex
7. Dad

A. 'Ah ha! Don't give up so easily.'
B. 'The Perception of Imperceptible Things'
C. 'I think we've got a poltergeist'

D. 'That's strong magic indeed.'

E. 'To the kitchen with these.'

F. 'Can you reverse the spell that did this?'

G. 'Messing about in my shop. Get out.'

INTERESTING VOCABULARY TO CRACK!

When reading, do you sometimes find a word grabs your attention because it is powerful or interesting? You can be on the lookout for these extraordinary words, and use them in your own writing! Here are a few interesting words used in this book.

gaunt – thin, lean and desolate in appearance

'He stood, tall and **gaunt**, in his corner.'

nymphs – in mythology, beautiful goddesses who lived in woods and near rivers.

'I came out in the grand, marbled lobby supported by pillars sculpted with **nymphs** and fauns.'

tyrant – a cruel and oppressive ruler

'Cesare was a complete **tyrant**: he tore the curtains, scratched the furniture, weed on the carpets and even chewed up my school project.'

monotonously – something lacking in variety and interest

'In the shadowy, aquarium, fish sailed **monotonously** back and forth in illuminated tanks.'

alabaster – a white stone usually carved into ornaments

'I still loved Franklin's, inside and out, for looking like something out of a fantasy novel – all that marble, **alabaster** and gilt.'

nanosecond – one thousand-millionth of a second

'I shuddered and thought for a **nanosecond** about telling my family.'

insubstantial – flimsy, not very solid or strong

'Some of the visible animals were a bit faded, not exactly transparent but sort of. . . weirdly **insubstantial**.'

sauntered – walked in a slow, relaxed way

'At that moment Cesare **sauntered** in and leapt lithely onto the bench.'

surreptitiously – in secret and so as not to be discovered

'I **surreptitiously** glanced round the kitchen.'

eloquently – spoken in an articulate and clear way

'Mr Walter Franklin had **eloquently** persuaded the other board members to vote in accordance with his wish to sell the Emporium.'

pugilism – the profession or hobby of boxing

'So fierce had the **pugilism** become that another board member summoned the police.'

imploded – collapsed inwardly

'Mum seized the other one and they propelled me away as the whole installation **imploded**.'

décor – furnishings and decoration

'I'd never taken any notice of them before; I'd thought they were part of the **décor**.'

ABOUT THE AUTHOR: GILL VICKERY

- *The Ivy Crown* was her first novel. It won an award: The Fidler First Novel Award.
- Gill has had many different jobs including teacher, nurse and packer in a chocolate factory.
- She has written six DragonChild books.
- Gill has loved writing and painting since she was small.
- Gill has also been a children's librarian. She says that it is the best job in the world as you get paid to read children's books!

WHAT NEXT?

If you enjoyed reading this story and haven't already read the first one – *Franklin's Emporium: The White Lace Gloves* – find it, snuggle up somewhere and READ IT!

Why not try writing your own story about invisibility or about a mysterious magician? Let your imagination run wild, but if you're a bit stuck, here are some starting points:

- An invisible animal causing trouble in a different place – maybe a school, or on holiday, or any situation you can dream up!
- Another story involving the liftman – what adventures does he have when he's not operating the Franklin's Emporium lift?

ANSWERS TO QUIZ

1d, 2a, 3e, 4g, 5b, 6f, 7c